D0347495

OXFORD
UNIVERSITY PRESS

Great Clarendon Street, Oxford OX2 6DP

Oxford University Press is a department of the University of Oxford.
It furthers the University's objective of excellence in research, scholarship,
and education by publishing worldwide in

Oxford New York

Athens Auckland Bangkok Bogotá Buenos Aires Calcutta
Cape Town Chennai Dar es Salaam Delhi Florence Hong Kong Istanbul
Karachi Kuala Lumpur Madrid Melbourne Mexico City Mumbai
Nairobi Paris São Paulo Singapore Taipei Tokyo Toronto Warsaw

with associated companies in Berlin Ibadan

Oxford is a registered trade mark of Oxford University Press
in the UK and in certain other countries

Illustrations copyright © Korky Paul 1989
Text copyright © Peter Carter 1989

The moral rights of the author and artist have been asserted

First published 1989
Reprinted 1990, 1992
First Published in paperback 1991
Reprinted 1994, 1996, 1998, 1999

All rights reserved. No part of this publication may be reproduced,
stored in a retrieval system, or transmitted, in any form or by any means,
without the prior permission in writing of Oxford University Press.
Within the UK, exceptions are allowed in respect of any fair
dealing for the purpose of research or private study, or criticism or
review, as permitted under the Copyright, Designs and Patents Act 1988,
or in the case of reprographic reproduction in accordance with
the terms of the licences issued by the Copyright Licensing Agency.
Enquiries concerning reproduction outside these terms and in other
countries should be sent to the Rights Department, Oxford University Press,
at the address above.

This book is sold subject to the condition that it shall not, by way of trade or
otherwise, be lent, re-sold, hired out or otherwise circulated without the
publisher's prior consent in any form of binding or cover other than that in
which it is published and without a similar condition including this condition
being imposed on the subsequent purchaser.

British Library Cataloguing in Publication Data available

ISBN 0-19-272230-1 (paperback)

Printed in Hong Kong

For Zoë: KP

Captain Teachum's BURIED TREASURE

Korky Paul and Peter Carter

Oxford University Press

Oxford Toronto Melbourne

Captain Teachum was a pirate.
He said.
He was the wickedest pirate
in the world—he said.

He attacked castles.

He captured ships.

He burned down whole towns.

And he made people walk the plank—he said.
He was the terror of the seven seas.

He buried his treasure.
He said.
He buried his treasure in ruined castles.

He buried his treasure
on desert islands.

He buried it in jungles—he said.

He buried it in the South Pole.
He buried it all over the world—he said.

He buried it in the North Pole.

But Captain Teachum had three secrets.
His wife made him do the washing-up!

He had *twenty-five* children!
And he had an awful memory, so . . .

He couldn't remember where he had buried his treasure!
He looked everywhere.
In the ruined castles,
on the desert islands,
in the jungles,
at the North Pole and at the South Pole.
But he couldn't find it anywhere!
So . . .

Maybe the treasure is still there.
Maybe . . .
He said.